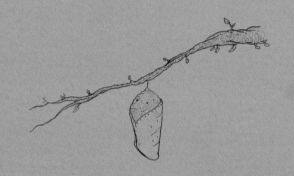

Presented to

_____

by

_____

on

_____

Good Night Tales

C. S. FRITZ

NAVPRESS

A NavPress resource published in alliance
with Tyndale House Publishers, Inc.

NAVPRESS ®

NavPress is the publishing ministry of The Navigators, an international Christian organization and leader in personal spiritual development. NavPress is committed to helping people grow spiritually and enjoy lives of meaning and hope through personal and group resources that are biblically rooted, culturally relevant, and highly practical.

For more information, visit www.NavPress.com.

Good Night Tales: A Family Treasury of Read-Aloud Stories

Copyright © 2017 by Casey Fritz. All rights reserved.

A NavPress resource published in alliance with Tyndale House Publishers, Inc.

NAVPRESS and the NAVPRESS logo are registered trademarks of NavPress, The Navigators, Colorado Springs, CO. *TYNDALE* is a registered trademark of Tyndale House Publishers, Inc. Absence of ® in connection with marks of NavPress or other parties does not indicate an absence of registration of those marks.

Scripture quotations marked NLT are taken from the *Holy Bible*, New Living Translation, copyright © 1996, 2004, 2015 by Tyndale House Foundation. Used by permission of Tyndale House Publishers, Inc., Carol Stream, Illinois 60188. All rights reserved. Scripture quotations marked NIV are taken from the Holy Bible, *New International Version*,® *NIV*.® Copyright © 1973, 1978, 1984, 2011 by Biblica, Inc.® Used by permission. All rights reserved worldwide.

The Team:
Don Pape, Publisher
Caitlyn Carlson, Developmental Editor
Dean H. Renninger, Designer
Eva Winters, Letterer

Published in association with DC Jacobson.

For information about special discounts for bulk purchases, please contact Tyndale House Publishers at csresponse@tyndale.com, or call 1-800-323-9400.

Cataloging-in-Publication Data is available.

ISBN 978-1-63146-556-7

Printed in China

23	22	21	20	19	18	17
7	6	5	4	3	2	1

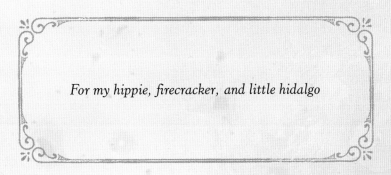

For my hippie, firecracker, and little hidalgo

CONTENTS

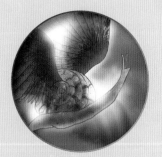

FOREWORD

I love children's books. As a father of three and a grandfather of nine, I have done more than my share of both reading children's stories and inventing a few of my own. Not to mention my assignment as a pastor to occasionally gather the children of my congregation to sit on the carpet for a story.

One of my favorite of these experiences happened in March one year as the snow melted and spring was on its way. I had brought an old bird's nest into the sanctuary and invited the preschoolers to join me for a story. When they were assembled, I showed them the nest. As we all huddled over it, I told them that a bird in Venezuela, a country a long way away in the south, had woken up that morning and realized that he and his friends could fly north and come to Montana for the summer. We talked together about how far it was and what the birds would do when they got to Montana, what trees they would nest in and what food they would eat. Then suddenly, one of the five-year-olds, Brucie, interrupted me: "Why don't you have any hair on your head?"

So much for visual aids. It took a while to get the children to refocus on the bird's nest.

My friend Casey Fritz is a dad and also a pastor, and he writes stories for children. This quite glorious book is full of interesting characters. My favorite is a plum-eating giant, but you and your children will be captured by all of them: a wolf and a fox and rabbits, lions galloping with deer, mice on the noses of bears, and turtles carrying beetles and worms on their shells. The final section concludes with a reassuring go-to-bed question to our King: "Do you love me?" The answer? Yes, yes, he does.

Eugene H Peterson

EUGENE PETERSON

TO THE READER

The imagination of a child is a thing of wonder, isn't it?
Children see the world in living color. Rain is music. Fingers are
paintbrushes. Meals are a palette. Every wall is a canvas.

Above all, children have an incredible mind for story. They see
a world brimming with possibility. Any given moment of their day
could be prefaced with "Once upon a time . . ."

We never quite lose that connection with story as we grow
older. No matter our age, stories can be transformative, a way of
expanding our imaginative borders, driving us to explore and reach
for heights unseen.

You hold in your hands twelve stories that point to the Grand
Story—God's redemptive story, the truest and greatest of stories.
Its wonders fill oceans. These stories will capture your imagination,
but they're not meant to leave you there. As you read stories of trolls

and treasures, crickets and songs, I hope you'll see the Grand Story running under them and stretching beyond them.

At the beginning of each story is the reference to Scripture that sparked my imagination, and at the end of this book are some questions to help you draw your children into conversations about the character of God and the reality of his grace. As you read these stories and questions together, I encourage you to listen to your children's answers rather than offering your own. See how their understanding grows each time you return to the story.

We all have been given an incredible ministry and opportunity to point the precious children in our lives to the one who made them and loves them. And story—the richness of imagination—can be a way to lead them there.

I pray that you connect deeply with the children in your life through these pages. But above all, I pray that they are drawn to the glorious King who is calling their names as you seek him together.

C. S. FRITZ

Kings of the Forest

Do you remember a time when kings ruled the forest?

When the wilderness was not its own, and the mountains were reverent?

Dandelions bowed,

shadows brightened,

creatures sang,

and the forest brimmed with blossoms and gladness.

There was **the king who ruled the trees**, who smelled of red maple and whistled the most somber of melodies as he walked through the forest at dawn.

There was **the king of the flowers**, who was draped in delicate petals and strands of ivy and whose famous temper would change with the seasons. Flowers would blossom or wilt depending on his mood.

There was **the mountain king**, who ruled over the peaks and hilltops that stretched far and long throughout the forests. When the clouds rained, the mournful king would cry into the night with the voice of thunder.

Every king in the land was powerful, but only one was glorious.

His name was so pure that no creature or tree dared to pronounce it. He was the King over all the other kings, and everyone—from the leaf beetle to the hare to the buffalo—bowed down to him. He spent long days roaming the land, talking with animals of all sizes, helping the weak, and guiding the strong. He loved all the creatures in his realm. And as the sun was setting by the great waterfall in the White Willow Gully, he could often be found singing to any animal that was near.

He truly was the greatest of the kings.

All the kings worked together to care for the forest, making sure the trees shaded the deer and the bees fed the flowers. But one year, when winter hung on just a little too long and its cold winds wouldn't retreat, something terrible happened.

In the White Willow Gully, all the creatures of the wilderness gathered before their glorious King.

"If you were truly a great king, you would stop this winter!" cried the toad.

"We no longer want to hear your songs," squawked the birds.

"We want a king like the others," lowed an elk.

The glorious King, with sadness in his heart, gave them what they asked for. He turned and left the forest.

Day after day the animals searched for a new king. They wanted a king that was not only like the others in the forest, but better.

They found him waiting in a dark and mysterious corner of the forest. He hibernated in the Bitternut Caverns every season but winter. *This bear was a ferocious, powerful, dreadful being.*

"He is strong!" whispered one fox to another.

"All the other kings will fear him," said the mountain lion.

The animals asked him to be their leader. The beast was only too happy to oblige. His time had finally come.

But even though the new king looked strong, he was secretly fearful and weak. His fierce anger made every creature tremble. He forced them to labor day and night to build and to hunt for him. *And winter after winter, his reign only grew worse.*

Over time, he began to worry about losing all that he had been given. He loved his treasure more than the four-horned antelope, his power more than the swallowtail butterfly . . . and himself more than the most fragile of elfin owls.

Soon his prideful heart filled with darkness, and he came up with a plan that would ensure that he—and he alone—would be king of the entire forest.

So on a night when the moon was bright and the stars were alive,
he took his lantern to the center of a tulip field. And while the earth
was asleep . . . **he let his lantern's flame run free.**

Every tree, shrub, and orchid burned into the air. The wilderness, which was once rich with life, was now filled with death.

When the other three kings saw that life in their kingdoms was no more, they blew a mournful kiss to the ashes and journeyed south. They were never seen again.

For centuries, the beast ruled an empire of embers and black wood. The day he finally died, all life in the forest was truly gone.

Until . . .

the glorious King returned.

In the midst of smoke and ash, the glorious King promised
that he would restore the wilderness, that he would bring
the caterpillars and the leaves back to life. . . .

And he would make all things new.

And he did. Creatures are coming from the north and south; leaves are opening on the branches of this wild wood; flowers are blooming up through the ashes.

And what once was a broken world is being made new. . . .

Of Trolls and Treasure

This is Purnice.

He's a buttonbush troll.

Buttonbush trolls are the groundskeepers of the forest.

They wander the wilderness, making paths for the waterfalls and waking the hibernating bears.

On this particular morning, Purnice discovered something *amazing*.

A cocoon.

And what was so special about the cocoon?

It was hiding a butterfly. The first butterfly, to be exact.

No one had seen a butterfly for hundreds of years. Everyone thought they were all gone . . . until now.

This cocoon must be cared for and loved, Purnice thought. He would give anything for this cocoon.

But there are rules in the forest. You can't just go around taking things that don't belong to you. And this particular cocoon was attached to an old maple stump.

That meant one thing.

Purnice needed permission from the Lord of the Trees to take care of the cocoon. He found the Lord of the Trees planting seeds by the river.

"Your Highness," Purnice said, "I am Purnice, a simple button-bush troll. I have just discovered the first cocoon attached to an old maple stump, deep in your trees, resting in a grassy field. May I take care of it?"

The Lord of the Trees stared at the buttonbush troll.

"What will you give me for it, troll?" he asked.

"Your Highness, you may have all of my fox eggs and the frogs I carry in my pocket," Purnice offered.

The Lord of the Trees thought for a moment. "I'll allow it," he said at last. "But you must also ask the Queen of the Field, for she owns the field where the stump lies."

Purnice walked far beyond the mountains toward the little valley among the high trees where he would find the Queen of the Field.

"Your Highness," he said, bowing in fear. (Everyone knows that trolls are dreadfully afraid of snakes.) "I am Purnice, a simple buttonbush troll. I have just discovered a cocoon attached to an old maple stump, deep in the trees, resting in your grassy field. May I take care of it?"

The Queen of the Field glowered at the buttonbush troll.

"Sssssssspeak up, creature. What did you ssssay to me?" hissed the queen.

Purnice closed his eyes and made his request again.

"Nothing isssss free, creature," said the queen. "What will you give me for the butterfly?"

Purnice thought carefully. "Your Highness, you may have my cottage home. It's not much, but what is there, I happily give to you."

"Then the bug is yoursssss," said the queen. "But you musssssst also assssk the Emperor of the Eassssst."

Purnice left the queen and traveled to the forest's swamplands.
The fireflies led Purnice directly to the *Emperor of the East.*

"Your Highness, I am Purnice, a simple troll. I have just discovered a cocoon attached to an old maple stump, deep in the trees, resting in a grassy field here in the east. May I take care of it?"

The Emperor of the East chuckled. "Well, if it isn't a little buttonbush. A cocoon, hm? What if I want to keep it for myself? Maybe I want to eat it! Have you had butterfly wing soup? It's delicious!"

"Please, Emperor," cried the troll. ***"I'll give anything for it."***

"Anything, huh?" the emperor said, smiling cruelly.

"I don't have much, Your Highness, but I promise to give you—" Purnice searched his mind. He had given all he had to the others! Finally he thought of it—"my year's wages."

"Deal! Mighty foolish if you ask me, buttonbush," said the emperor. "But you must also ask the glorious King."

Purnice walked into the high mountains, through cold streams and fierce winds, until he came to the court of the glorious King.

"Glorious King, I am Purnice—"

"I know who you are, my dear Purnice," the King said. **"Ask of me what you wish."**

"Well . . . I have discovered the only cocoon attached to an old maple stump, deep in the trees, resting in a grassy field in the east. I would like to take care of it."

The King stroked his golden beard. "This means a lot to you, doesn't it, Purnice?" the King asked.

"Yes, glorious King," said Purnice. "I'd give my life up for it."

"Then it is yours," said the King.
And Purnice ran back to the forest to find the most
important treasure in the world.

PSALM 23

A Sheep's Journey

Once upon a meadow, the Barrhead sheep and their lambs set off in search of a new home. Barrheads are the explorers of the wilderness.

They are brave sheep who walk over the highest rocks and through the darkest wolf dens. But that doesn't mean they are never afraid.

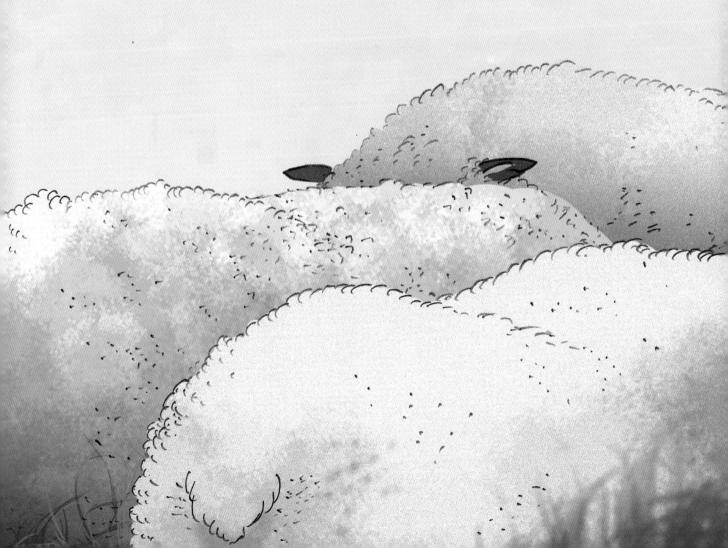

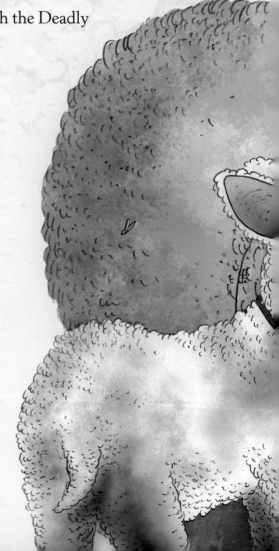

"*Where are we going today, Father?*" asked a lamb.

"I don't know for certain," replied his father. "But because the Shepherd is leading, it must be somewhere good."

"The others are saying we are going through the Deadly Valley!" cried the lamb. "Aren't you scared?"

"Of course I am! But do you see the Shepherd?" said his father. "He is our watchman, our guide, our fighter."

"So he is all we need?" The lamb stared at the Shepherd and his wooden staff.

"He is all we want, and more than we need," his father said. "More than the quiet streams he leads us to drink from. And more than the green pastures he leads us to lie in."

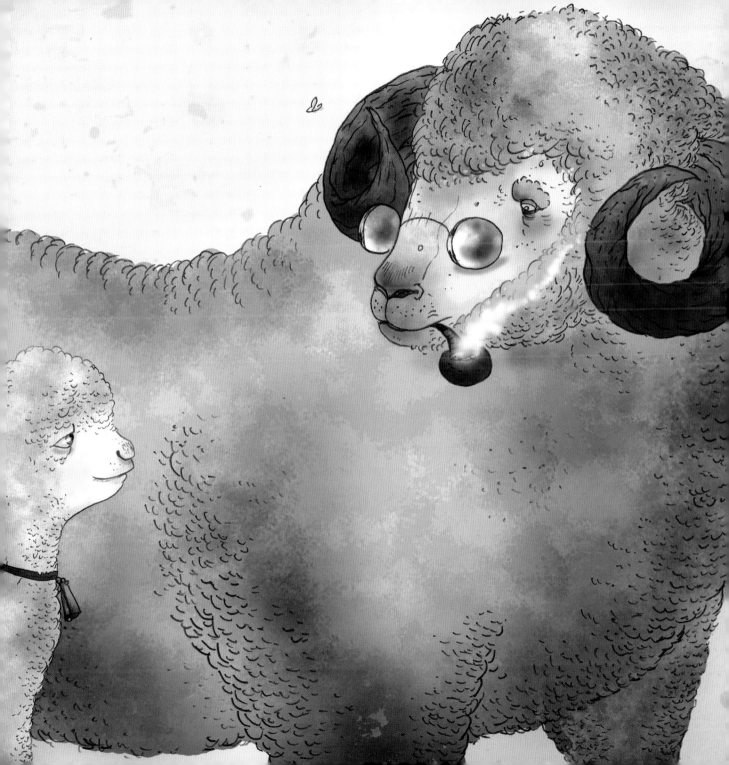

As the flock walked into the Deadly Valley, they could hear
the howling of wolves and the clicking beaks of the ravens.
Black thorns and thickets clung to the sheep and their young
as they passed. But the darkness was far worse than the thorns.
The sheep were unable to see their Shepherd.

"Father, may we please go back?" whispered the frightened lamb. When there was no response, the little lamb panicked. "Father! Where are you?"

The lamb ran deeper and deeper into the thickets, searching for his father. But the fog surrounded the little lamb, and suddenly two

flaming eyes stopped him in his tracks. The lamb tried to back away, but thorns wrapped and twisted around his hooves and snout.

The lamb was stuck.

All he could do was cry as the thorns grew tighter and the eyes came closer.

And just when the lamb had lost all hope, he heard something:
a song in the distance. As the melody grew louder and closer, the
thorns loosened their grip and the flaming eyes faded back into
the darkness.

The lamb knew the voice that sang.

It was the Shepherd, calling to his lost little lamb.

The Shepherd pulled the lamb from the thorns and held him
close to his heart. ***"Fear not, little one,"*** he said softly, ***"for I am
with you."***

He gently carried the lamb back to the flock. The lamb's father
rejoiced to see his lost son return.

And then the Shepherd lifted his lantern and led the flock out of
the Deadly Valley and into the land of Goodness and Mercy, where
they dwelled together forever.

THE

Extraordinary Ordinary Snail

"I once crafted a vessel with my bare hands!"

said the snail. "I navigated across the forbidden sea, over black waves and under gray skies, and I feared I'd crash against the horned rocks— but I didn't! Would you say that makes me a captain, buffalo?"

"No," said the buffalo as he munched on some grass. "I saw you—you simply perched on a birch leaf during a rainy afternoon. You're ordinary and very small—and you don't have hands."

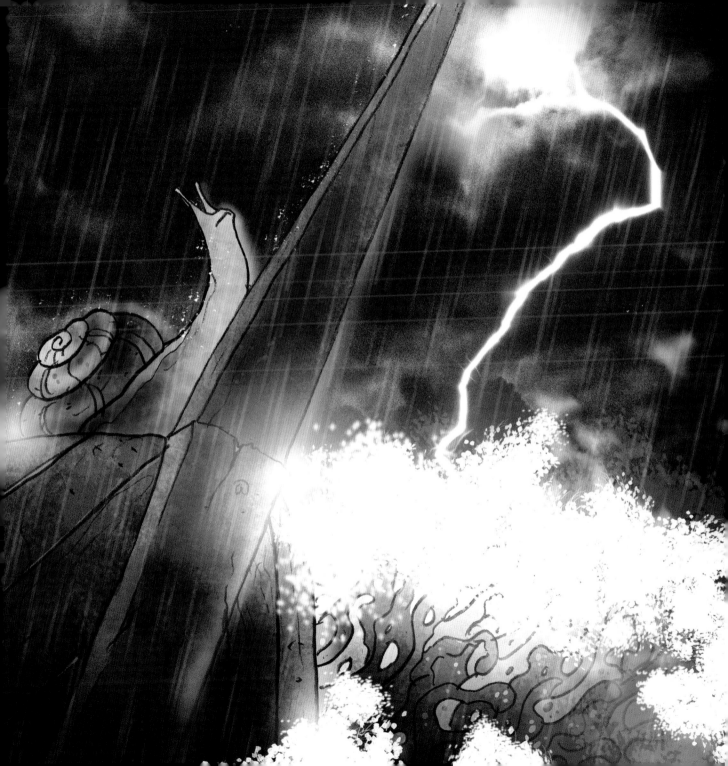

The snail stood tall and said, "Once I had the wings of a wildwood eagle and soared through the rainbows, through colors that have only been seen in heaven. Do you think that I am special and was the only one to see it?"

"No," said the buffalo. "I saw you—you were just sitting in a field of wildflowers. ***You're ordinary and very small***—and you don't have wings."

"Well, buffalo, do you remember my hike to the summit of the largest mountain?" asked the snail.

"It was a rock, and it took you all morning," snorted the buffalo.

"What about the time I found a dragon?" shouted the snail.

"Duck," the buffalo corrected him. "Face it, snail, you're nothing. How sad it must be to be a snail, to be so ordinary."

The snail said with all the courage he could gather, "You're wrong—even though you are large, truly the size of the moon compared to me. You can go wherever you want, when you want, yet you somehow still see the wilderness as you see me—ordinary and small.

"But let me tell you: **The glorious King made me just as I am,** and that means being ordinary is the most extraordinary thing in the world."

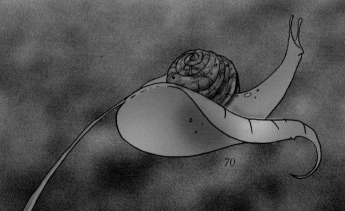

70

The Song of the Cricket

Instruments don't make beautiful sounds.

Those who play them do.

The same piece of willow wood and silver string can be dreamy or piercing. Don't listen to the sound—listen to the heart. The heart of the musician makes the music.

Just ask Merton Sourwood.

Merton Sourwood played his fiddle in the village on the edge of the forest. He didn't have socks or blankets, but he did have his fiddle. He played that fiddle every morning and every evening by the fountain near the bakery. And as he played "Geese in the Bottle" and "Dancing on the Moon," the village children laughed and danced in the cobblestone streets.

But then one day the cricket came to town.

The cricket played a song so beautiful, hundreds of people came to hear him play. No one listened to the fiddle of Merton Sourwood. And this bothered Merton very, very much.

"I play my fiddle for this town," Merton said to the cricket. "No one is listening to me now that you're here!"

"I mean no offense," the cricket said. "I love to play my fiddle."

But Merton wanted to be liked just as much as the cricket was. He wanted all the people to come listen to him instead.

As Merton's heart grew more envious, the sweet sounds of his fiddle became shrill. Even the local brown cow could moo a better tune.

It's that cricket's fault my fiddle is screeching! Merton Sourwood thought. So Merton made a plan.

One night while the cricket was asleep, Merton crushed his tiny fiddle.

In the morning, Merton tuned his fiddle and laid out his hat in hopes of a shilling or two. Now that the cricket could not play his fiddle, Merton thought everything could go back to the way it was. So Merton lifted his fiddle, breathed in, and began to play.

But to Merton's surprise, he had not gotten better. He had gotten far, far worse.

The townsfolk fled the streets, shut their windows, and clenched their teeth. Merton's song was so sour, no one wanted to listen.

Merton's heart broke.

But then he heard something amazing.

The cricket was standing next to Merton, using his own two legs to play a beautiful harmony with Merton's song.

All of Merton's jealousy faded away. The cricket was helping him play music, even after Merton had broken his fiddle? Merton's heart grew bright because of the cricket's love, and his music became more beautiful than ever.

Merton Sourwood may not have had socks or blankets, but he did have the cricket's forgiveness. *And from that day forward, the two of them played music together.*

The Good Mouse

LUKE 10:25-37

93

THE
Wood Elf
Who Wouldn't

Every creature in the wilderness has a job to do.

The buttonbush trolls wake the hibernating bears.

The foxes hang the beehives.

And the wood elves tend the trees.

Well... most of them do.

Caring for the trees is an important job.

Trees need quite a bit of care, and all the wood elves work hard to watch over their own trees.

They paint the leaves with the colors of autumn, and they take the leaves off one by one to prepare for winter.

They never forget to clean out the robin's nest, and they always, always offer the owl a cup of herbal tea. (Owls are grumpy if they don't get their tea.)

But one particular wood elf wanted nothing to do with it.

He wanted to nap all day and spend his afternoons eating beetles.

On one of those afternoons the Lord of the Trees visited the little wood elf.

"You slothful little elf!" exclaimed the Lord of the Trees. "What have you done with yourself? You are treating this opportunity as a nuisance! Until you learn your lesson, I am taking your job away."

"I don't care," scoffed the wood elf. **"I don't want to work."** And he crawled back into a pile of leaves and fell asleep.

So when spring came, the other elves spruced up their trees with new blooms. As they carefully pulled each bud open, the slothful elf watched from his resting spot, happy not to have a reason to get up.

As spring turned into summer, the little wood elf watched the skin of his tree turn gray and slowly peel away. The wood elf's tree had died. At first, the wood elf was happy. This meant more naps in the sun and more beetles in his belly.

But soon the wood elf began to get lonely. The robin stopped landing on his branches, and the owl found tea somewhere else. As he watched the leaves fall from the other trees, his heart fell with them. And as he watched the other wood elves work hard for their trees, he realized they weren't doing it for themselves but for every creature in the forest.

The wood elf realized that without his help, his tree would have no life—and if his tree didn't have life . . . well, in a way, neither would he.

"Please, Lord of the Trees, allow me to work for you once more!" cried the elf. *"I miss the owl. I miss the robins. I miss the colors of spring and fall. I miss my job!"*

The Lord of the Trees smiled. "Very good," he said. "I am glad you have seen the importance of the tree you have been given. Go and bring life back to your tree, my little wood elf."

The wood elf worked very hard. He sometimes got tired, but he never gave up. And finally, after many springs, life came back to the wood elf's dead tree.

The little wood elf ran to the Lord of the Trees. "I have grown the tree and doubled its branches! Now there are robins and magpies and golden finches!"

The Lord of the Trees opened his arms wide. *"Well done, wood elf.* I am proud of the work you have done, and I am giving you more trees to take care of as a reward. *Come . . . let's celebrate!"*

LUKE 15:3-7

The Toy

JOHN 8:1-11

THE
Plum-Eating Giant

Do you know about the giant that sleeps
just beyond the edge of town?

Myths of old tell of giants that thrashed and smashed, but the truth is, **giants are more scared of you than you are of them.**

And if you ever want to make friends with a giant? Just give 'em a plum.

Giants can't resist the taste of plums, especially Black Amber plums.

And there is only one orchard in the whole village—and in the whole forest!—where plums grow.

Old Mr. Friar's orchard.

But Mr. Friar doesn't like to share.

Unfortunately, the giant that sleeps beyond the edge of town can't read.

Early one morning, Mr. Friar poured a cup of cream for his cat and a cup of tea for himself. Mr. Friar likes to drink his tea while looking out his eastern window and admiring his orchard. Only this time, there was no orchard to be seen. Or sun, for that matter. Only a shadow. A giant shadow, to be exact.

Mr. Friar and his farmhands grabbed some rope and snuck up behind the giant. They tossed the heavy rope over and under the giant until he couldn't move!

"Throw him over the waterfall!" Mr. Friar shouted.

They dragged the poor giant through the pasture, past the butcher's house, and straight on through the forest. As they went along, more and more townsfolk joined in to help.

The giant was scared—and frankly, still hungry!

As Mr. Friar began pushing the giant toward the cliff's edge, someone shouted from the crowd.

"Papa! Don't!"

Mr. Friar stopped. It was his daughter, Violet.

"This doesn't concern you, Violet!" he said. "Go home!"

But Violet wasn't about to leave. She pushed her way through the crowd until she got to the front.

"But he just ate a plum!" she said. "Papa, everyone eats our plums! Mrs. Handley," she said, turning to the baker, "haven't you eaten plums from our orchard? Or you, Mr. Elwood? Mr. Sourwood, I saw you bite into a plum yesterday. Yet we'll find fault in this giant before we do in ourselves? Papa, we are all just like this giant."

Everyone in the crowd started looking at their feet. They had all eaten plums from Mr. Friar's orchard even though they knew it was wrong. They began to go away one at a time until only Violet was left with the giant.

The farmer's daughter loosened the ropes and asked,

"Giant, where are they? Do you see anyone left?"

"No," whispered the giant, wiping the tears from his eyes.

"Neither do I," she said. "Now, let's go get you a plum."

Fell into the Earth

132

137

GENESIS 7:1-5

The King Is Calling

"Drop everything! We need to leave at once," said the husband.

"What? What do you mean? I just put dinner on," said the wife.

"This is more important than dinner," he said.

"You're scaring me," she said. "Where have you been?"

"I've heard from the King. He called my name. We need to leave . . . now!"

"The King spoke to you?" The wife was skeptical. "The King hasn't spoken in a hundred years."

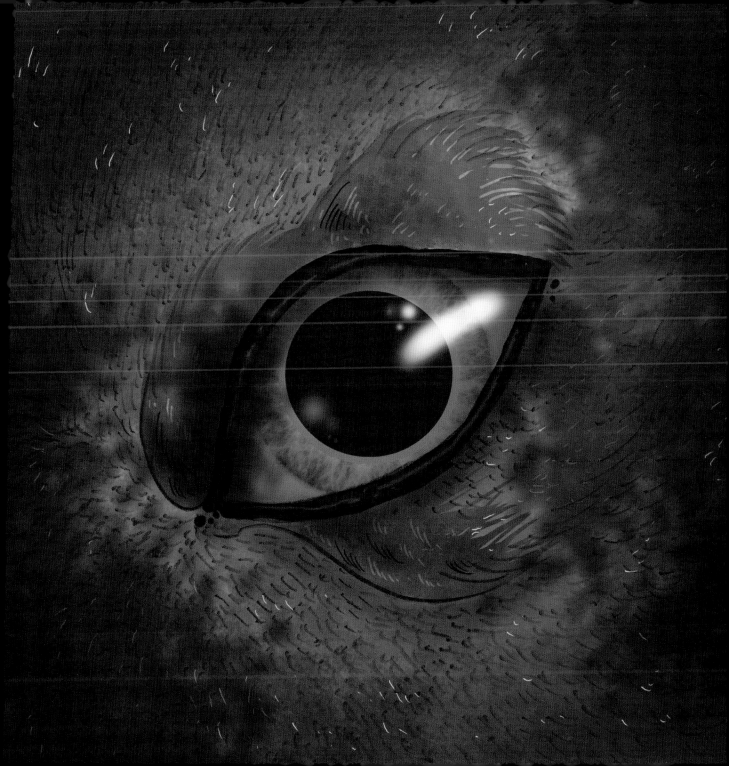

"Where did he tell you to go?"

"North. And after that . . ." The husband shook his head. "I don't know."

"North?" she cried. ***"Are you crazy? Do you know the monsters that live in the north?"***

"I do. That's why I feel we must go. Only for the King would I be willing to do this."

"Are we in danger?" the wife asked.

"Well, yes . . . no . . . not really." Again he shook his head. "I don't know."

"Then I must warn the others."

"That'll do no good," he told her. "They will not come. The King told me so."

"I'm starting to not like the King," the wife said. "Why can't the others come? We have to tell my mother and sisters, my nieces and nephews. And what about the sparrows, the moles, and the beetles? Can't I tell them?"

"Wife, I am sorry. But we must trust the King."

"I'm scared, Husband."

"I am too."

"Quiet. . . . Do you see it?" the wife whispered.

"We must keep going if we're going to make it north by dawn," he whispered back.

"It's looking right at us," she said.

"What? What is?"

"The wolf."

"Yes, now I see it." The husband shivered. "Listen, we'll run for that burrow in three, two . . ."

"Did he speak to you, too?" the wolf shouted at the rabbits.

The husband and wife looked at each other. "Is he talking to us?"

"Did the King speak to you rabbits?" the wolf asked again. "To head north?"

"Yes!" the husband said.

"Why are you talking to that wolf?" The wife cringed.

"He knows something!"

"It's all right—you can come out," the wolf said. "We don't want to hunt you. We are going north."

"We are too," the rabbits said.

"Are you alone?" the wolf asked.

"Yes. Are you?"

"Heavens, no. My wife is with me . . . but so are all of them."

The valley was filled with creatures. Lions galloping with deer, mice on the noses of bears, and turtles carrying beetles and worms on their shells. "They're all marching north, just like you, and just like me."

"What is going on, wolf?" the husband asked.

"Life will soon be no more," the wolf said gravely. "The King is taking it."

"But why? But how? The King is supposed to be good and right," the wife said.

"Who are you to question the King, small rabbit?" asked the wolf. "Are you not one of his creations? Do you know his intentions and thoughts? The King knows what is good, does what is good, and is good. It's life that is no longer good."

"It's just hard to understand," she said.

"For all of us," the wolf said.

"I can't believe this is the end." Tears filled the wife's eyes.

"No, rabbit, not the end," the wolf said softly. ***"The beginning."***

Do You Love Me?

156

"Do you love me?" asked the sparrow.

"Look at the sun," said the King.

"Each day I wake her and put her to sleep. Not a minute too soon, and not a minute too late.

"It is the same sun, yet each day she casts new shadows and blooms new flowers.

"Whatever the night may bring, my sun scrubs it away.

"Surely you must know my love from the sun?"

"But the sun leaves me once a day. *Are you saying your love will leave me?*" asked the sparrow.

"Do you see the mountain?" asked the King.

"Have you ever seen it change or move?

"It is like my love, which is the same yesterday, today, and forever.

"I love you when you doubt, fail, and lie. Nothing you can do will change my love.

"Surely you must know my love from the mountain?"

"But the mountain is so far away. *Is your love only for those who can climb its peak?*" asked the sparrow.

"Drink the rain," said the King.

    "Does it fall just on you? Or also on the bear and the snake?

    "I love equally and show no partiality between predator and prey.

    "I am fair in my love just as I am in the rain.

    "Surely you must know my love from the rain?"

"But this is so hard to believe or know. ***Help my unbelief, King,***" begged the sparrow.

"Look at the stars," said the King.

"Do you see them during the day? Of course not! But they are still there.

"So it is with my love. Though you may not always see it, believe it, or trust it, my love—like the stars—is there.

"And not only is my love present, but vast.

"When life is at its darkest, my love will shine brightest.

"Surely you must know my love by the stars?"

"But, King, I am a fearful creature. How do I know you are capable of this love?" asked the sparrow.

"Do you see the moon?" asked the King.

"No one knows him. He shines his light when the forest sleeps.

"Yet each night he lights the land.

"Is not my love greater than his, as I give just for you with no expectation of return?"

"This love sounds as big as the sea, and I am so small. ***How do I know you love me?*** " asked the sparrow.

"Look at yourself, little sparrow," said the King.

"When you fall from a tree, do I not know it?

"Am I not there to mend your wing and sing you a song?

"My love is your own.

"I watch over you as if you were the only one."

"O King, I don't deserve this love. **You are too wonderful and too good,**" cried the sparrow.

"My sparrow, look at me," said the King.

"I am yours and you are mine.

"If you do not know my love by the stars or mountains, by the moon or rain, then surely you must know that you are loved, for I give you all I am.

"I love you with an unchanging love.

"So yes, my sparrow, I love you.

"More than you'll ever know."

⅏ GOING DEEPER: ⅏
DISCUSSION PROMPTS

Kings of the Forest READ 1 SAMUEL 8 TOGETHER.

1. The animals of the forest had a good and wonderful King. But what kind of king did they ask for? What happened when they got their new king? Why do people sometimes want things that are bad for them?

2. In the Bible story, the people of Israel had God as their one and only King. But like the animals in the forest, the Israelites also decided they wanted a different king. How do you think that made God feel?

3. The Israelites, like the animals, were stubborn and wanted to live their own way rather than live God's better way. Have you ever chosen your own way instead of God's? Why do you think God's way would have been better to follow?

4. Even though the animals were stubborn, the glorious King showed them grace and chose to return. Grace is when someone gives a gift that isn't deserved. Describe one way God shows you grace when you are stubborn.

Of Trolls and Treasure READ MATTHEW 13:44 TOGETHER.

1. In Jesus' parable, the man who found the treasure is a lot like Purnice, who found the cocoon. Both knew what they found was very precious and valuable. If you found something very valuable, would you want to keep it? If you could keep it, what would you do with it?

2. Jesus says that the treasure is actually the Kingdom of Heaven. The Kingdom of Heaven is the way in which God wants the world and our hearts to be—following Jesus! How precious and valuable do you think the Kingdom of Heaven is?

3. Purnice sells everything he has to gain the cocoon, and the man in the Bible sells

everything he has to gain the treasure in the field. Why is Purnice so eager to have this cocoon? What do you love so much that you'd give up anything for it?

A Sheep's Journey READ PSALM 23 TOGETHER.

1. Psalm 23 is a song about how God loves us. What part of this psalm do you like the best?
2. This psalm tells us that God is like a shepherd who takes really good care of his sheep—us! What are some ways in which he takes care of you and shows you how much he loves you?
3. This psalm compares God to a shepherd, but what else could you compare God to? Fill in this blank: God protects me and cares for me, just like _____.

The Extraordinary Ordinary Snail READ PSALM 139:14 TOGETHER.

1. The snail in the story sees the world as an amazing adventure. What is your favorite part of God's creation and why?
2. God made each of us in different and special ways. What is something wonderful that he made different and special about you?
3. The buffalo tries to tell the snail he's not special, but the snail knows the buffalo is wrong because the glorious King made him! Psalm 139 tells us everything God makes is wonderful. What can you say to encourage someone who feels small or unimportant?

The Song of the Cricket READ PHILIPPIANS 2:3 TOGETHER.

1. Merton Sourwood's music became worse because he was jealous of the cricket. We're no different! Being jealous of someone else only hurts us. How does it make you feel when someone is better than you? What can you do about that feeling?
2. What does the verse mean when it says to "value others above yourselves"?
3. The cricket decided to forgive Merton for breaking his fiddle and even help Merton

with his music. What are one or two ways you can show forgiveness and compassion to someone who has hurt you?

The Good Mouse   READ LUKE 10:25-37 TOGETHER.

1. The mouse in this story helped the owl even though the mouse had to go out into the cold to do it (and owls are scary to mice!). Sometimes loving other people is hard. Who is someone you have a hard time loving? Why?
2. The neighbor in Jesus' story was the man who showed mercy. Mercy means choosing to help other people even when they might be hard to love. How can you be a neighbor to the person you have a hard time loving?
3. Name three ways you and your family can show mercy to others who need help. Be brave and actually do these things together!

The Wood Elf Who Wouldn't   READ MATTHEW 25:14-30 TOGETHER.

1. This Bible story is another one of Jesus' parables that he uses to teach about God and God's Kingdom. He's reminding us that God wants us to use all the things he's given to us! What gifts and abilities has God given you?
2. The wood elf took his tree for granted and was happy to stop taking care of it. Sometimes we don't use God's gifts very well either. But God knows that we are happier when we take care of his gifts! How can you use the gifts God has given you?
3. When we use God's gifts well, God is excited to give us bigger opportunities! What do you dream about doing for God? How can your gifts help you do this?

The Toy   READ LUKE 15:3-7 TOGETHER.

1. When the toymaker realizes that one of his toys is lost, he immediately goes to find it and is so happy when he does. Have you ever lost something important to you? How did you feel when you found it?

2. Jesus tells us in his parable that God is very happy when a person who has been following his or her own way begins to live God's way again. What does it mean to be a "lost sinner who repents"?

3. If you have decided to follow Jesus, God is rejoicing over you! If you haven't, God is out looking for you like the toymaker in the snow. Do you have any questions about Jesus? Would you like to follow him?

The Plum-Eating Giant READ JOHN 8:1-11 TOGETHER.

1. All the people from the village thought they were better than the giant. The people in our Bible story were the same way! Look back at what Jesus said to these people in verse 7. What do you think he meant?

2. Jesus shows mercy to the woman in the story and rescues her. (Remember our definition of mercy? Mercy means choosing to help other people even when you have a hard time loving them.) What does he tell the woman to do after he saves her life?

3. Jesus also wants to give each of us mercy, no matter what we've done. But in order to turn to him for mercy, we have to turn away from our sin. What do you need to turn away from in order to turn toward his mercy?

Fell into the Earth READ JOHN 12:23-26 TOGETHER.

1. The Bible shows us that following Jesus means we may need to give up some things to follow his ways. But whatever the cost is, God's reward is greater! What was the reward for the farmhand in the story when she finally let go of the special seed?

2. There is no bad deal with Jesus! God might ask us to do something hard, such as making wise choices or being nice to someone who is mean, but his reasons are always good, even when we don't understand. What is a hard thing God wants you to do that you haven't done? What is keeping you from doing what God asks?

3. Our Bible verses say that if we give God what is most precious to us, he will use it in amazing ways. For the farmhand, the seed was her precious possession, and giving

it up meant that the seed could become a forest of trees! What is something most precious to you? How do you think God could use it?

The King Is Calling READ GENESIS 7:1-5 TOGETHER.

1. Imagine you were one of the animals that God wanted to go on the ark. How do you think you would have felt? Would you have been excited? Scared?
2. The rabbits leave everything behind to trust the one who is calling them, just as Noah and his family trusted God as they built the ark. When is it easy to trust God? When is it hard?
3. The rabbits say that God is good, even in the hard times. As a family, make a list of all the ways God has been good to you and place that list where you all can see it. Whenever you discover another way in which God has been good to you, add it to the list!

Do You Love Me? READ 1 JOHN 4:7-19 TOGETHER.

1. We read in our Bible verses today that we're supposed to love other people because of how much God loves us. Name someone you can especially love today. Name one or two ways in which you can show God's love to that person.
2. The little sparrow found it difficult to believe that the King truly loved her. But the King showed her through all creation that he did. Think back to your favorite part of creation. How does it remind you of God's love for you?
3. The King told the sparrow that he loved her because—along with the sun, mountain, rain, stars, river, and moon—he gave her himself. Jesus has done the same as the King. He gave you all of creation and gave all of himself to show you how deeply he loves you. Do you believe Jesus loves you? Because he does, more than you will ever know. Pray together, thanking him for his great love.